"I love this wonderful book. How does Mal Peet do so much in such a short space? It's engrossing, haunting, beautifully written" *DAVID ALMOND*

"A timely reminder of what a magician Mal Peet was. How you cast such a powerful, intoxicating spell with so few words is beyond me" *PHIL EARLE*

"For thoughtful, intelligent young readers, no writer of this century writes better than Mal Peet" *MEG ROSOFF*

"I commissioned *The Family Tree* for an anthology I was editing for Walker Books, and I knew as soon as Mal sent it to me that it was a great story – full of the warmth and insight into people that was so characteristic of Mal as a writer and a human being. I'm really pleased to see that it's being issued as a book in its own right by that most excellent publisher Barrington Stoke – and I'm very moved that Mal dedicated the book to me and to Gill Evans, the editor I was working with at Walker Books. Mal is very much missed – but at least we still have his stories to read" *TONY BRADMAN*

"A story of such challenging emotional complexity, yet told so simply, so gently. No wonder Mal Peet is a story-teller we miss so much" *KEITH GRAY*

THE
FAMILY
TREE

THE
FAMILY
TREE

MAL PEET

Illustrations by
EMMA SHOARD

Barrington Stoke

First published in 2018 in Great Britain by
Barrington Stoke Ltd
18 Walker Street, Edinburgh, EH3 7LP

www.barringtonstoke.co.uk

A CIP catalogue record for this book is available
from the British Library upon request

ISBN: 978-1-78112-805-3

Printed in China by Leo

To Gill Evans and Tony Bradman

1

I was shocked. No, upset. Like when you upset
a glass or something, and everything spills out.

I thought, 'The New People haven't looked
after it. How could they have let it get into this
state?'

Then I thought, 'It's probably not the same
New People. We left here almost twenty years

ago. My God. The house could've been bought and sold any number of times since then.'

And then I thought, 'You shouldn't have come back. You should never go back.'

*

In fact, I hadn't intended to. It's just that I was driving past the end of the lane, coming back from a job, and decided to come and have a look. I hardly ever find myself in this part of the world. So let's call it a whim. Let's not say that it was as if another hand, an invisible hand, had reached across and turned the wheel.

There's a little pull-in fifty metres or so past the house. Trees, half-bare, and beyond them a ploughed field, regular as corrugated cardboard. I parked the van and got out. There was a squashed KFC box and two Sprite cans in a puddle. I walked back to where I could see into our old garden without being seen from the house. There's a long black railing that separates the garden from the lane. The big old – no, ancient – beech tree is at the far end of the railing. It stretches some of its arms across the lane. I'd driven under them. It stretches others towards the house, over the lawn. The Nest is built into these branches.

What am I saying, is built?

My dad built it. It took him weeks. Or months. Time's bendy when you're little.

THE FAMILY TREE

I stood there looking at the scruffy

wreckage in the tree's lower branches, hanging

there like a mishap.

2

"Now then, Benjamin," Dad said. "That is what you call a tree. A serious tree."

I picture myself holding his hand and looking up. I wish I could remember myself. What I was wearing, and so forth. But I can't. The tree was a huge grey tower holding its canopy of pale-green leaves up against the sky. The sun kaleidoscoped light through it. Behind

us, Mum's voice was telling the removals men

where to put things.

Dad let go of my hand and put both his

hands on the trunk of the tree and looked up

into it.

"Yes," he said, as if he was talking to Mum.

"Hmm. I think so. This will do nicely."

3

So, when Mum was onto him to do other stuff,

Dad spent time building me a treehouse. He

built a platform about three metres above

the ground, nailing things together in a

complicated way, sawing bits of wood into

angles, fixing them together. He'd apologise to

the tree every time he hammered a nail into it.

Then a floor, walls, and a roof that he covered

with gritty black stuff to keep future rain out.

He took the ladders away and built a flight of
steps up to the first fat horizontal branch, then
another up into the back of The Nest. (That
was its name. Dad had carved it into a little
wooden board nailed above the entrance.)

I remember the day he fixed the last step
into place. I was looking up at him. He climbed

back down without looking at the ground. I
thought, 'I'll never be able to do that.'

"Stay here," Dad said, and went back to the
house.

I stood there while the sky went pink.

Something swiftly shadowy above me
screeched.

He came back loaded up – a sleeping-bag, sandwiches in a plastic box, a can of Coke and candles in his pockets, a bottle of wine under one arm, a pillow.

"Come on, then," he said, so I followed his confident arse up the steps.

We stepped into the treehouse. One end of it, the end we faced, was a big window with a door in it. The door opened onto a little balcony with a rail and balusters made of sawn branches. My dad was magic to have created such a thing. The landscape unfolded itself into the distance, layers of green and brown and

lavender with the last light of the sunken sun beyond it. The air smelt of sap and clean wood, with a slight whiff of cow manure.

Dad drank wine from the neck of the bottle and wiped his mouth with the back of his hand.

"What do you think of your nest?"

I thought it was wonderful. Outrageous.

I said, "Is it for me?"

Dad looked at me, frowny-smiling. "Of course it is," he said.

*

THE FAMILY TREE

I fell asleep by candlelight, thinking, trusting,

that he would carry me back down and across

the lawn and up the stairs and to my bed via

my mother's kiss. But he didn't. I woke up

feeling cold, then panicky.

Dad put his hand on me, saying, "Shush, Ben. Listen. The dawn chorus."

I needed a pee. The birds sounded as anxious as my mother.

4

I was nine years old. Ten, that summer.

Me and Dad spent evenings in The Nest,

lighting candles against the dark. He'd made

improvements, as he called them. A shelf for

books. Hooks on the wall for our coats and his

binoculars. A nifty little plywood box with a

rope handle where we stashed our 'essentials' –

two plastic plates, two knives, two forks, a

bottle of water, his Swiss Army knife with the corkscrew, my comics.

He read me *The Wind in the Willows* and *Tom's Midnight Garden*. I loved it all so much. Some nights, The Nest would shift and creak as the old beech adjusted itself to the weather.

And I wanted to say, after that first time, "Let's stay here, Dad. Let's sleep here."

But he would say, "Don't be daft, Ben. Mum'll be wondering where we've got to. Come on."

And down we'd go. And when we went into the house Mum was usually on the phone.

That's how I remember it, anyway.

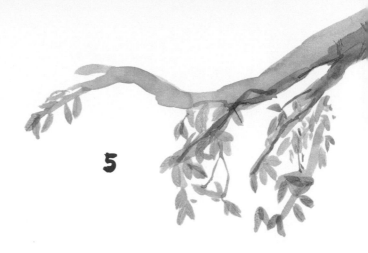

5

Months went by. Christmas, then Easter. I think

we'd lived in the house for almost exactly a year

on the morning I went downstairs for breakfast

but instead of the usual radio and the hiss of the

kettle and Mum and Dad talking about what was

going to happen there was only Mum standing

in front of the kitchen window with her arms

folded. When she heard me, she turned round

and I saw that she was smoking a cigarette.

"Where's Dad?"

"Up that bloody tree of his," she said. "Get your clothes on and tell him that breakfast is ready and that he's got a bloody job to go to."

*

There was the kind of low mist that hangs on to your legs, but I left it behind on about the fourth step up to The Nest. Dad was sitting cross-legged on the sleeping-bag staring out of the window.

I could see, and smell, that he'd slept the night there. At the time, I felt cheated rather than worried.

"Wotcha, Ben."

"Hello, Dad."

The mist rolled away into the distance. You couldn't say where it ended and the sky began. The trees looked like they'd been painted onto the landscape, then blotted before the paint had dried.

Dad said, "It's like flying, sitting here, don't you think? Like the mist is clouds and we're above them."

He stretched his arms out and rocked them gently, like a coasting bird. He had his eyes closed.

I said, "Mum says breakfast is ready and that you've got a bloody job to go to."

He didn't answer.

After a while I said, "Dad?"

He nodded his head and said, "Yeah. I heard you."

He carried on nodding his head as though he had no control of it.

"Dad?"

He looked up at me, just for a second, and I saw that he was crying. Not making any noise, but tears running down his face as steady as water from a tap. I didn't know what to do, so I was glad when Mum's voice cut through the moment.

"Sean? Sean! For God's sake! For God's sake!"

*

I wasn't clever enough, or perhaps just not old enough, to work out what was going on. And anyway, when you're young you're so wrapped up in yourself, aren't you? Everything that happens to you is so important, so absolutely unique and brightly lit. Parents are just wallpaper. The background.

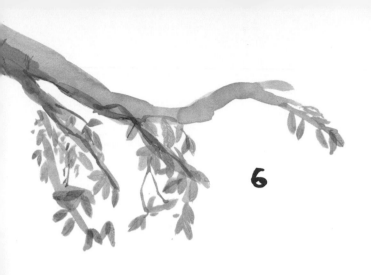

6

Summer came round again, like the quick hands of a huge clock. The school holidays. It didn't seem odd that Dad also stopped work. We'd gone away in the summer, the years before that year. To Auntie Jan's in Cornwall. Or on planes to Spain or Greece. But that year we didn't go anywhere. Nothing was planned or talked about. Mum carried on going to work. Dad and I messed about in the garden or went to the supermarket in Okehampton or did

bits of work on The Nest. Sometimes on hot

afternoons we would lie on our backs on the

lawn and repeat the stories that the passing

clouds told us.

THE FAMILY TREE

Mum came back later and later, usually when Dad was asleep in front of the telly. I'd see the lights of her car rake the windows and then hear her tyres brake on the gravel and then I'd go up to bed before she fumbled with the door latch.

MAL PEET

I didn't want to hear what they said to each
other, her kind of angry and him mumbling and
sort of laughing like he was telling bad jokes.
Once, though, there was a row. Shouting. I
wanted to go down because my head was full
of the word *please*, but didn't. It went on a

THE FAMILY TREE

long time, starting up again when I thought
it was over. Then I heard Mum come upstairs
and use the bathroom. I was rigid in the dark,
listening. She opened my door but I kept still.
She sort of sighed my name then went to the
bedroom.

I waited for Dad to come up, but he didn't. After a while I heard the back door open and close. I counted to a hundred then tiptoed down the corridor to the spare bedroom, stepping carefully over the floorboards that creaked. The window looked over the lawn. The black lump of The Nest in the beech tree had a yellow rectangle drawn on it. Dad's candle, showing through the narrow gaps around the door. The full moon hung in the branches above him like an escaped balloon.

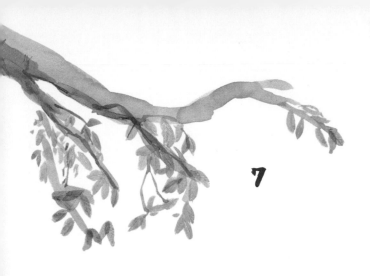

7

Everything fell apart that summer, after Dad

moved into The Nest, but the strange thing

is that I remember being very happy most

of the time. In my memory, it never rained

or got cold, although I suppose it must have

done. I think of it as a gold and green time. I

had breakfast with Mum most days, and she

was usually chirpy and busy like a nervous

bird. Then the phone would ring and she'd

say "Hi" in a warm voice and take it into the hall, leaving her cereal to go soggy in the bowl. Fool that I was, I thought at first that Dad had secretly rigged up a phone in the treehouse. Then I started hearing her say "Steve".

A routine established itself. Mum would leave for work, leaving a trail of instructions in her wake. Then I'd get dressed and carry the carton of Sugar Puffs and a bottle of milk over to The Nest. Sometimes Dad would be awake, sitting up in the sleeping-bag and reading one of my comics. Sometimes I'd have to wake him up. While he slurped the sweetened milk I'd tell him the things that Mum wanted us to do.

Some mornings he'd say, briskly, "Right. Right."

Other mornings he'd say, "Aw, do we have to do that, Benjie? I don't really wanna do that."

*

Dad stopped cooking. He'd been really keen, watching food programmes on the telly, making notes, sometimes going all the way to Exeter to buy weird bits and pieces from the Lebanese shop or the market. He'd take forever fussing over pans on the stove. He bought a set of square plates and put the food on them like it was an abstract painting or something. He gave all that up after he moved

into The Nest. At five o'clock or thereabouts

we'd go into the kitchen and make beans on

toast with a fried egg on top. Or fish finger

sandwiches, or cheese on toast with crispy

bacon. We'd scuttle across the lawn and carry

these greasy feasts up into the treehouse as if

somebody was out there trying to stop us. The

Essentials Box now contained brown sauce and

ketchup, and always, mysteriously, at least one

bottle of wine.

One evening, the sun a red bubble

sinking towards the horizon, Dad lifted his

egg-and-ketchup-smeared plate to his face and

licked it clean like a dog. I was shocked and

thrilled.

He looked at me and said, with a serious

smile on his face, "Don't try this at home."

8

The winter loomed in and slowly faded away.

One morning in spring, when the mud in the

lane had more or less dried out and the verge

in front of the house was mad with daffodils,

a man in a suit and wellies came and put up a

To Let sign on a post just inside the railings.

By the time I got home from school Dad had

sawn the post off close to the ground and

thrown the sign over the hedge into the field

opposite. I made two mugs of tea-bag tea

and carried them over to The Nest. Dad was

sitting on the balcony with his legs through the

balusters, reading a book and chuckling. He

turned and looked up, showing me. The book

was old and its dust-jacket was torn but I could

read the title – *Biggles and the Cruise of the Condor.*

"I read this when I was your age," Dad said. "I'd forgotten how brilliantly mad it is."

He hadn't shaved for about a week. His hair was quite long now, and his face had got harder and sharper. His nose was beaky.

"Mum'll play hell when she sees what you did to that sign," I said.

He stuck his bottom lip out and shrugged.

"See if I care," he said.

*

Mum did play hell. She parked fiercely on the gravel and didn't come into the house. I heard the boot-lid of her car slam. I went to the living-room window. Mum was marching across the lawn with a torch in her hand, following an oval of light that made the grass white. At the foot of the beech tree she aimed the beam up at The Nest.

"Sean! Sean!"

It was a screech.

"Sean, you pathetic bastard! Come down from there!"

The Nest remained silent.

"Sean! I know you can hear me, you shit! How long do you intend to maintain this, this fucking charade?"

I pulled the curtains across the window and turned the volume on the telly up. After a while I heard the door slam and a chair scrape on the kitchen floor. I went through and Mum was sitting with her hands flat on the table either side of the big black rubber torch.

She looked up at me and said, "I'm sorry, Benjie. I'm really sorry."

I shrugged and said, "It's all right."

"I never meant this to happen. I love this house."

I didn't say anything. I hadn't imagined that what was happening was to do with the house. I thought it was something else.

The phone rang. Mum sort of jumped but didn't answer it. After eight rings the answer machine clicked in. A man's voice said, "Helen? Call me. I'm worried."

"Was that Steve?" I asked her.

Mum took a deep breath as if she was smoking an invisible cigarette.

"Yes. You'd like Steve. He's very normal."

"What does he do?"

Mum looked at me as if I'd asked a very weird question. Then she laughed, sort of.

"I'll tell you what he doesn't do, Benjie. He doesn't live up a bloody tree."

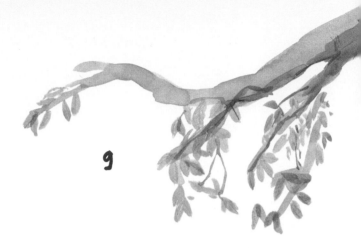

9

Over the next few weekends people came to

look at the house. Some of them brought their

children. Most of them were impressed by The

Nest and wanted to go up into it.

"No," Mum would say. "I know it's lovely

but the floor isn't safe. If someone fell through

it and hurt themselves, well, we're not insured.

If you take the place on, well, that's up to you."

And half of me wanted my mad dad to hurl the door open and throw his dirty underpants down at the strangers, and half of me was praying that he wouldn't because it would be so awful for Mum.

*

We packed everything back into the same boxes we'd come with. The removals men were like a comedy act. They couldn't say anything that wasn't a joke. When they'd gone, Dad was still in The Nest.

Auntie Jan poked her ciggie into the gravel with her toe.

"Right then," she said.

She and her partner Joe, a big bearded man, and my dad's two brothers, Uncle Liam and Uncle Frank, walked across the lawn towards the big old beech tree. They looked like a showdown gang from an old Western. Liam had a crowbar, brand new from B & Q, in his hand. Dad didn't answer them when they called up to him, so Liam climbed the curved steps round the tree trunk to the door of The Nest and forced it open with the crowbar.

I sat in the back of Steve's BMW, watching.

They brought him down. He looked all around as though he was considering flight but couldn't think how to manage it. When he got his feet onto the ground, his knees buckled and Joe hoisted Dad's left arm round his shoulder and sort of carried him over to the drive.

Dad didn't look that upset. His beak poked out between the curtains of his hair and his eyes were wide, like someone who'd woken up somewhere surprisingly beautiful. He was wearing shorts and flip-flops and a T-shirt with a Snoopy cartoon on the front. They took him

to Joe's car, passing the BMW. Mum sobbed and fell sideways onto Steve's shoulder.

He reached an arm around her and said, "It'll be all right, babe. It'll be all right."

I twisted to look through the rear window and saw Uncle Frank put his hand on the top of Dad's head, like a policeman, to guide him into Joe's car's back seat.

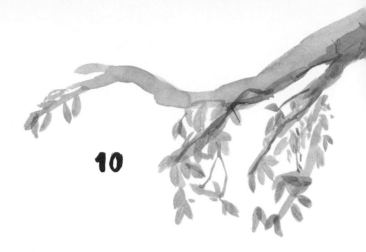

10

I stood in the lane staring at the wrecked

treehouse for, I don't know, five minutes,

maybe longer. The roofing felt had split

and peeled and the plywood underneath was

rain-stained and buckled. The wall-boards had

gaps between them, and were greeny-black

with slime and something like soot. The

whole structure had slumped, tilted. It looked

accidental, half-hearted. The bottom four steps

had gone and the rest were skewed and rotten. It was a disgrace.

For the first time ever I felt ashamed of my dad. Or of myself, or both. It made me angry. I'd marched up the short drive and knocked on the back door before I'd thought about what I might say.

A woman about my own age opened the door. She had one of those nice harmless faces that you forget soon afterwards. She was very pregnant, which put me off my stroke a bit. It took me several seconds to get my first words out. Anger makes my stammer worse, anyway.

I suppose it would have made things easier if I'd introduced myself but I was too worked up to think of it.

When the words eventually came, they came in an ugly blurt. About how I used to live here I was just passing my dad built The Nest he lived in it for a year I was shocked to see the state it was in.

I could see she hadn't understood. And that she was a bit frightened. I may have sounded aggressive. She put her hands over her big bump.

She said, "The nest?"

"Yes," I said, and pointed meaninglessly towards the lawn. "The Nest. The treehouse."

"Oh," she said. Then, without taking her eyes off me, she turned her head slightly towards the hallway behind her and called out, "Gareth? Gareth!"

I looked down at my shoes for a bit and when I looked up there was a man standing behind her. He had a child, a boy, three years old perhaps, hanging off him. The boy had his arms hooked around his dad's neck and his bare legs clamped on his dad's hip. The kid was whingeing quietly – "Dad-dee, Dad-dee."

The man said, "Hi. Can I help you? Are you selling something? We don't want any plastic windows."

And right then I knew what I wanted to tell them. Which was, that I'd come and fix The Nest up for them. In my summer holiday. I'd like to. For free. No strings attached. It would be nice for the kid. Kids. A place like this cries out for a treehouse. I'd bring my own food and everything. I wouldn't bother them.

I was looking at the man's face while the pictures of all this came into my head. I'm not good at telling people's ages, but I'd've said he was a few years older than his wife. I saw that there was tiredness in and around his eyes. I saw that he was jigging the little boy up and down automatically, unconsciously, the way that animals in a zoo do the same thing over and over.

Something inside me gave up, folded.

"No," I said. "It's all right. I'm sorry to have bothered you."

*

I went back to the van and picked the junk-food carton and the two cans out of the puddle and put them in the plastic carrier-bag that contained the remains of my lunch.

I sat quietly behind the steering wheel for a minute or so until I felt OK then I made a three-point turn in the lane and went back the way I'd come.